CRADDOCK
ELEMENTARY SCHOOL —

All of us are good at some things
and not so good at others — and
that's okay. We don't have to be the best
or good at everything we do.

Enjoy whatever you are good at and
share this "gift" with others. This type of
sharing is what makes you a little different
from others — and being a little different
is not only "cool" but it is special!

Fran Gonsales
Gonsales

DISCARD

DONATED

W9-BDB-960

ZOLLIE GOES WEST

by Gary Consilio

Illustrated by Andrea Karcic

2004 First Edition

© 2002 Gary Consilio
Edited by Diane Nickle
ISBN 0-9742623-0-7
Library of Congress Number 2003096032

All Rights Reserved.

Submit all requests for reprints to:

SAFARI EXPRESS

P.O. Box 25592
Garfield Hts. Ohio 44125
(216) 272-5050
Website: www.zollie.net <http://www.zollie.net>

No part of this publication may be produced, stored in a retrieval system,
or transmitted in any form or by any means, electronic, mechanical, photocopying,
recording, or otherwise, without the prior written permission of the publisher.

Printed in China

To Victoria Ciofani-Consilio - Thank you for your amazing love, devotion, trust, and respect. You truly are "my" Victoria!

◆ ◆ ◆

In memory of my mother, Incornata M. Consilio, who passed away September 21, 2002: You are the most loving, compassionate person I have ever known. I want to thank you, Mom, for a lifetime of unconditional love, understanding, patience, and encouragement. You are the best!

◆ ◆ ◆

In memory of my father, Gus J. Consilio, who passed away March 15, 2003: Thank you for an amazing childhood and your belief in my ability to succeed at anything that I tried. You helped instill in me a high level of confidence and self-esteem.

◆ ◆ ◆

Among the people closest to me, while I was working on "ZOLLIE GOES WEST" was Helen Garonzi's three year old (at the time) son, Matthew. Among our favorite activities besides going to the Cleveland Metropark Zoo and Six Flags, was to read books together. It didn't matter how many times we read the same books, using countless different voices, animation, and even changing the stories as we went, it was always a very special time for the three of us. Thank you Helen and Matthew.

◆ ◆ ◆

Thank you to Gina Smigel at GNL Signs & Graphics for doing an amazingly awesome job of converting my Jeep Wrangler into Zollie's Personal Vehicle. The children absolutely love it!

◆ ◆ ◆

A special thank you to Andrea Karcic (my illustrator), who amazingly captured my mental image of the main characters and "brought them to life." Your sense of humor, creativity, and artistic genius are without limit.

◆ ◆ ◆

A very special thank you and my sincerest gratitude to Lisa Umina, author of the highly acclaimed "MILO WITH A HALO" and the soon to be released, "MILO'S MOMENTS." You are a very special friend as well as my "consigliere." Your love and passionate commitment to children is not only a bond we share, but a driving force behind what we do. You inspire me to look even deeper within myself to find a way to touch people's lives and to truly make a difference. Thanks Lis!

◆ ◆ ◆

And most importantly … Thank you, God, for blessing me with a talent and guiding me in how best to use it!

ABOUT ZOLLIE

Zollie the zebra was created to teach valuable life lessons to our children. The zebra, possibly the most highly recognized animal that exists today, shares obvious similarities and differences with other animals. In doing so, Zollie makes for a fun and an easy segue to a discussion about people. Zollie succeeds in providing an entertaining and simple introduction to our own diversity and an individual's self-worth. Zollie dislikes the term "tolerance" which falls drastically short of his goal which is understanding, respect, and acceptance.

INTRODUCTION

"ZOLLIE GOES WEST" is the first of a planned series of children's books that provides an entertaining way to teach and reinforce vital life lessons. It can be a very effective educational tool in the hands of parents, grandparents, teachers, etc., especially when introduced to children in their early school years. "ZOLLIE GOES WEST" addresses the similarities and differences between us and ultimately reveals and defines the worth of each individual.

As adults, we need to do a better job of instilling in our children the ability and the willingness to respectfully interact with people, regardless of social, cultural, religious, or political differences.

We can no longer neglect the responsibility, nor assume these lessons will be taught and learned, unless each of us shares in this obligation. In doing so, this will help our children develop, at an early age, a better understanding of their eventual role in an ever-changing global society.

Hopefully, this understanding will help prevent a repeat of the devastatingly horrific Holocaust, the tragic events of September 11th, and the continuation of racial prejudice. More than ever, we all owe this to our children as we try to prepare and assist them in their integration into the world community.

Hello, my name is Zollie and I am a zebra. I'm two years old in zebra years which makes me six in people years. I live on the plains of Africa among many different types of animals including elephants, giraffes, monkeys, hippos, lions, and more. Although I live amongst a variety of animals, sharing food and water, I stay close to my own herd, so I don't get lost or in trouble. Being a young male zebra, I spend a lot of time each day doing zebra stuff like eating grass, taking dust baths, running around kicking up my heels, and playing rough and tumble with the other guys in the herd. I also love to sleep and take naps in the shade, lying on my side.

Before I get carried away talking about myself, I would like you to meet my family. I live with my father and mother, Zach and Zelma Zebra. Mom and Dad spend their time protecting and taking care of the family. I also have a younger brother Zeus and a younger sister Zeena. We are a close family and like to do many things together, such as play tag and splash around in the lake. Our favorite family activities include watching old movies and reading stories together. Mom and Dad taught us the importance of family and they have always encouraged us to spend time together. Although sometimes a younger brother or sister can be annoying, Zeus and Zeena do look up to me and that makes me feel good. They enjoy the stories that I read to them and when they get a little older, I'll teach them to read so they can explore the world of books on their own.

Although I look like any other young zebra, I am different in a very special way. I have an incredible imagination. I can go anywhere that I want just by closing my eyes and concentrating on a place I want to visit. Then, just for fun, I say some special words while I spin around in a circle. My imagination never seems to fail me. I love going to different places, and wherever I go, I make new friends. For me, every trip is an adventure.

When I'm not doing zebra stuff, I often get ideas of new places to visit by going to the library. The library has books about everything. The more books I read, the more I learn, and the reading helps my imagination to grow. My library is just like yours, except everything is bigger and everything is outside.

Before I go to the library, I always get permission from my mom and dad, so they know where I am. As I headed off to the library, I decided to look at books about the western part of the United States. I got this idea from watching movies about horses and donkeys from the "Old West." These horses and donkeys looked a bit like me, except without the "cool stripes." As I continued to browse through the books, I came across a place called "Wally's Western World." It was a western ranch with cowboys, cattle, and cacti, but more importantly, there were also horses and donkeys.

A visit to Wally's Western World would surely be a fun way to meet different animals from another part of the world. As my curiosity continued to peak, I knew I was ready for my trip.

     With a destination in mind, I closed my eyes and began to think about my new adventure. I was concentrating real hard, spinning in a circle while saying the special words:

I AM A SPECIAL ZEBRA
AND MY NAME IS ZOLLIE,
I REALLY LOVE TO TRAVEL
AND I'M OFF AGAIN,
BY GOLLY!

Once I stopped spinning, my eyes widened as I realized I was standing at the entrance to Wally's Western World. I didn't see any other zebras, but I did see cows, sheep, goats, chickens, dogs, and even buffalo.

My interest continued to build as I watched the other guests arrive. Suddenly, I was face to face with what I thought was a zebra covered in mud and dust. But as I looked closer, I realized that this was not a zebra. This guy was grayish brown in color, about the same size as me except thinner, and had much bigger ears. "Hi, I am Danny the donkey. I live on a small farm and my job is to plow fields and haul heavy loads of vegetables to the marketplace. The farmer and his wife are good to me. They appreciate all my hard work and, to show their thanks, they sent me on vacation to Wally's Western World. I'm anxious to meet everyone and hopefully, I'll make some new friends." As I looked him up and down, it was obvious that we were a lot alike. We were similar size, similar shape, but as for color … well, maybe Danny wouldn't look good in stripes.

I told Danny that I was a zebra from Africa and excited about my new adventure. We continued to talk about where we came from and our families until we were both distracted by another arrival. He looked magnificent. He was very tall and muscular and looked real important by the way he pranced up towards Danny and me. He was a brown and white painted horse with a long flowing mane. Everyone around us also admired this horse and they cleared a path as to acknowledge his greatness. "Hello, I am Herbie, and as you can see, I am the star of this gathering. I live on a big farm where I have the best of everything. I live in a huge stall, eat the finest food, and have plenty of room to run and play with my friends. I'm not really sure why I came here, except for being curious to see how the rest of you live, *especially you guys*," as he pointed to Danny and me. Danny and I introduced ourselves and said that we were also curious. Herbie said, "I've been told by others that we are a lot alike, but when I look at Danny, all I see are your long silly-looking ears, and as for you, Zollie, what's up with the stripes? Oh well, enough about you … just follow my lead and maybe we will chat later."

After checking in, Danny and I talked a while longer and we were getting along fine. We decided it would be fun to go on the trail hike to Gopher Gulch with the other guests. Before the hike began we were divided into groups of three, so Herbie, Danny, and I were a team. Herbie put himself in charge because he told us that he was quite knowledgeable of trails, had great speed to scout ahead, and because he felt he was a born leader. As we prepared to leave, Danny and I loaded our supplies that consisted of mostly food and our tents. Herbie was racing around and showing off how fast he could run. With his long slender legs, running very fast was easy for Herbie.

Not long into the hike, Herbie started to complain that Danny was too slow. Herbie liked to brag how fast he could run. He would take off real fast and then wait around the next bend in the trail for us to catch up to him. Danny, who was used to carrying heavy loads, was not impressed with Herbie's actions. He felt it was wiser to save his strength for the long hike ahead and besides that, Danny and I were carrying Herbie's share of the supplies. I knew that Danny was right, but nothing we said would convince Herbie to slow down.

GOPHER GULCH
7 MILES →

The next hour was more of the same until the trail brought us to the bottom of a very steep hill. One by one, everyone caught up to Herbie who was passing his time taking a nap under some trees. As Herbie continued to sleep, we all passed him by and proceeded up the hill.

When we got to the top, Danny and I unloaded the supplies and started to set up camp when we realized that Herbie still was not around. After searching the campsite, we were unable to find him and it was getting dark. While the others were relaxing from their strenuous hike and getting ready for dinner, Danny and I started back down the hill in search of Herbie. I went first because zebras can see really well in the dark and Danny was close behind me.

About half way down the hill, Danny thought he heard something. As he turned his big ears back and forth, he finally was able to figure out where the sound was coming from. As we headed in that direction, I began to see a familiar face just ahead of us. It was Herbie. As Herbie explained what happened to him, we realized that instead of climbing the hill slowly and carefully like everyone else, he was more concerned with being the fastest and got his hoof caught in a gopher hole. Herbie was glad to see us and even happier once we freed his leg.

When the three of us finally made it to the top of the hill, it was time for dinner. We were all very hungry and the grass, hay, and oats all tasted delicious. After a long drink of water, Herbie thanked us again for coming to his rescue. He told us that when he first got stuck, it was no big deal to him. He figured he would work his leg free and then race up the hill, laughing at everybody, as he passed them by. After all … he was Herbie.

But as the hours passed and it was getting dark, Herbie became afraid, realizing that his great speed and bragging could not help him out of trouble. The more he thought about it, the more Herbie realized just how wrong he was, and how poorly he had treated all of us. Herbie wanted the others, especially Danny and me, to come look for him, even though Herbie only cared about himself. It finally began to make sense to Herbie, that to make friends, you have to be a friend. And to be a friend, you have to try to understand others; to accept them as they are and to respect them … no matter what.

Even though Herbie was faster and taller, Danny was stronger and could hear the whisper of the wind. I was strong, but not as strong as Danny. I was fast, but not as fast as Herbie. But I can see really well in the dark and besides that … I have stripes!

The more we talked, the more we realized that even though we are spotted and striped, taller and shorter, fatter and thinner, have big ears and little ears, long legs and short legs … we have some differences, but we are the same in many more ways. Herbie, Danny, and I discovered that we are all very special. We are special because of the many talents that we have and how we share these talents with others. *It is not based on the way we look.*

It was getting late and time to get some sleep, because in the morning we would continue on our trail hike. Tomorrow would be easier and more fun because we knew that Herbie would carry his share of the supplies and he would be content to walk together with his two new friends.

I was happy that all of us, especially Herbie, learned something very important on this trip. Herbie learned what it means to be a true friend, and how important it is to accept and respect others. As for me, I'm glad we all don't look and act alike. What a boring world this would be if we were all the same. If we take the time to get to know each other, it will be a lot more fun and easier to make new friends.

The sound of the bells in the library startled me. I opened my eyes and realized that the library was getting ready to close. It was time for me to go home. I can't wait to tell Zeus, Zeena, Mom and Dad about my adventure to Wally's Western World.

On my way home, I thought about my trip and the valuable life lessons I had learned. Friends come in all different sizes, shapes, and colors. We all have strengths and weaknesses and we don't have to be the best at everything. What matters is that we all try a little harder to get along, to understand and respect each other. We all deserve this because each and every one of us is an important part of this world. If we all really try, together, we can make our world a much better place for all of us to live.

EARN YOUR STRIPES

Zollie wants and needs ...

You to make an
Obligation to better
Understand and
Respect others.

Hello or Hi is a good 1st step.
Easier than you think – Just try!
Look for a chance to know someone better.
Perfect? None of us are. Be accepting.

Hey Guys ...

Did my book help you to make a new friend?
Did my book help you to better understand or respect someone?
Did my book help you to appreciate someone different than you?
If you answered yes, write me a letter and tell me how my
book has helped you.

Join my "Earn Your Stripes" Club

Mail your letter to:

SAFARI EXPRESS

"Earn Your Stripes"
P.O. Box 25592
Garfield Hts., Ohio 44125-5592